SITTIN' IN with the BIG BAND

jazz ensemble play-along

Track 1: tune to B♭ concert.

	Page #	Demo track	Play-Along track
Vehicle	2	2	3
Sax to the Max	4	4	5
Nutcracker Rock	6	6	7
Fiesta Latina	8	8	9
Now What	10	10	11
Goodbye My Heart	12	12	13
Two and a Half Men	14	14	15
Burritos to Go	16	16	17
Drummin' Man	18	18	19
Swingin' Shanty	20	20	21
Play That Funky Music	22	22	23
Performance Notes	24		

How to Use This Book

Each arrangement has two CD tracks:
1) Demonstration track. The Alto Saxophone part is in the mix. Listen to how your part is played by professional musicians to copy the phrasing, intonation, articulation, feel, style, section/ensemble blend and concept.
2) Play-Along track. Your part has been taken out of the mix. You play-along with the big band.
3) See page 24 for Performance Notes
4) There is a two-measure count-off click at the beginning of each play-along track.

Alfred Publishing Co. Inc. thanks the students of
Mary Ward Catholic Secondary School Jazz Ensemble, Toronto, Canada,
John Volpe, director, Vince Gassi, assistant director, and photographers Jackie Fong and Jermaine Ong.

Alfred Publishing Co., Inc.
16320 Roscoe Blvd., Suite 100
P.O. Box 10003
Van Nuys, CA 91410-0003
alfred.com

A Division of ALFRED PUBLISHING CO., INC.

ISBN-10: 0-7390-4513-X

VEHICLE

By JAMES M. PETERIK
Arranged by RALPH FORD (ASCAP)

1st Eb Alto Saxophone

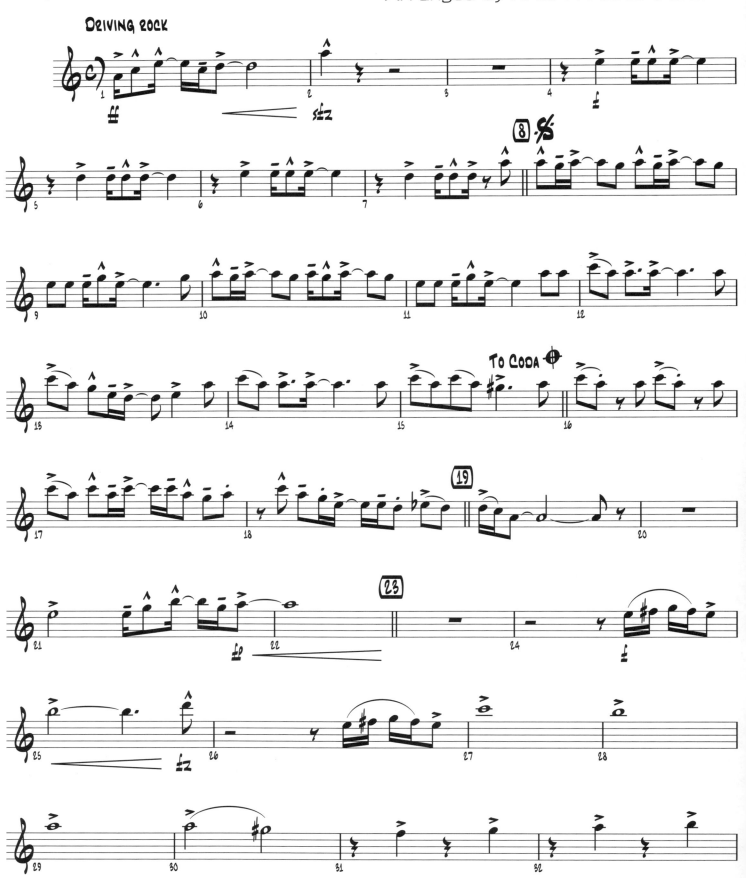

27527

SAX TO THE MAX

1st Eb Alto Saxophone

by MIKE LEWIS

Medium Swing

NUTCRACKER ROCK

By TCHAIKOWSKY
Arranged by MIKE SMUKAL

1st Eb Alto Saxophone

FIESTA LATINA

VICTOR LOPEZ

1st Eb Alto Saxophone

Latin

NOW WHAT

By MIKE KAMUF

1st Eb Alto Saxophone

27527

GOODBYE MY HEART

1st Eb Alto Saxophone

By MIKE SMUKAL

TWO AND A HALF MEN
Main Theme

1st Eb Alto Saxophone

Words and Music by GRANT GEISSMAN,
LEE ARONSOHN and CHUCK LORRE
Arranged by ROY PHILLIPPE

BURRITOS TO GO

1st Eb Alto Saxophone

VICTOR LOPEZ (ASCAP)

DRUMMIN' MAN

1st Eb Alto Saxophone

By GENE KRUPA and TINY PARHAM
Arranged by RICH DeROSA

27527

SWINGIN' SHANTY

1st Eb Alto Saxophone

TRADITIONAL
Arranged by RALPH FORD (ASCAP)

21

27527

PLAY THAT FUNKY MUSIC

1st Eb Alto Saxophone

Words and Music by ROBERT PARISSI
Arranged by VICTOR LOPEZ

PERFORMANCE NOTES FOR ALTO SAX

Playing 1st alto in a big band is a challenging but very rewarding job. Here are a few tips for playing lead alto in a big band:

- Focus on blend, intonation, articulation, phrasing, and playing with accurate time. In addition, listen to the lead trumpet and match the style, pitch, sound, and feel.
- Don't over blow on the loud dynamics because it may affect your intonation.
- Listen and fit your part on top of the section harmony.
- In a rock or Latin style chart, the eighth notes are played even, not swung.
- In a rock style arrangement chart carefully observe the rhythmic syncopation.
- Observe articulations and dynamic markings throughout the charts.
- Make sure you can hear the recording well so you can lock in your time and feel with the band.
- The marcato or rooftop accent (^) is played detached but not staccato, think "daht."
- Try recording yourself while you play along with the play-along track and see how close you can get to sounding like you are in the band
- Have fun being the "virtual" lead alto player!

There is a two-measure count-off click at the beginning of each play-along track

Vehicle:

1) In a rock style, eighth notes are played even, not swung so don't lay back—play with energy and forward motion.
2) In measure 38, listen carefully to the other alto sax and the trumpets and play the unison section with good intonation.
3) The quarter notes in measures 30–32 are accented and long, think "dah."
4) In measure 66, the trombone plays rubato and then the drumset plays a fill in-tempo to bring you in for the last two measures.

Sax to the Max:

1) Play the soli lines smoothly with an even sound.
2) As the lead alto, listen for your part on top of the section harmony.
3) The marcato or rooftop accent (^) is played detached, think "daht."
4) The last eighth note in a group is short.

Nutcracker Rock:

1) In this rock/march style, play the eighth notes even.
2) The marcato or rooftop accent (^) is played detached, think "daht."
3) In measure 41, play the unison line with the trumpet as one—listen!
4) Observe the articulation.

Fiesta Latina:

1) This Latin style chart has plenty of unison lines therefore good air support is critical to maintain accurate intonation. Listen and blend!
2) At measure 53, listen and match the articulation with the other instruments.

Now What:

1) Listen carefully in the unison lines with the alto sax and trumpets.
2) Observe the articulation.
3) At 54, solo the second time playing either the written solo or ad lib.
4) The chord changes provided have two chords: for the Bmi9 chord, use the notes of the A major scale and for the Cmi9 chord, use the notes of the B-flat major scale. They are both Dorian minor scales.

Goodbye My Heart:

1) For this solo ballad, maintain good air support which will help intonation and phrasing.
2) Relax and play with a full sound—avoid pinching the embouchure and tone.
3) Stay close to the written solo. You can take more liberties in measures 29–35.
4) Some vibrato is appropriate in this type of solo feature—but always in good taste.
5) Ballads look easy but require concentration. Tell a musical story!

Two and a Half Men:

1) At measure 17, listen and blend the unison lines.
2) The solo can be played as written or ad lib in the style of the chart.

Burritos to Go:

1) Play the marcato accents detached but not staccato.
2) The last eighth note in a group is short.
3) Play the solo as written or ad lib. Learning the notes in the chords and scales will help you navigate through the chord progression.

Drummin' Man:

1) This traditional swing style is concise and tight. Listen and match the articulation.
2) The last eighth note in a group is short.
3) As the lead alto, listen for your part on top of the section harmony.

Swingin' Shanty:

1) Play the eighth notes with a strong swing feel.
2) Solo the first time through the solo section at measure 51, play the background notes the second time. Play the solo as written or ad lib.
3) Learn the notes of the chords and scales in the solo section.

Play That Funky Music:

1) Observe the accents and articulation. Listen!
2) Play the two sixteenth notes with a "doo-dit" articulation.

Recorded at **Bias Recording Studios,** Springfield, VA
Bob Dawson, Engineer
Featuring the **Belwin Jazz Big Band, Pete BarenBregge,** Director.

Learn **jazz concepts, improvisation** and **sight reading** for all instruments
from jazz legend **Bob Mintzer!**

- **12 jazz etudes composed by Bob Mintzer in a variety of jazz styles, tempos, and time signatures**
- **Performance notes/tips for each etude to assist in interpretation and improvisation**
- **Play-along CD with a stellar rhythm section**
- **All books are compatible and written so they can be performed together!**

12 Contemporary Jazz Etudes
Book & CD

(ELM04011)	C Instruments—Flute, Guitar, Violin, Keyboards	$24.95
(ELM04012)	B♭ Tenor Saxophone and Soprano Saxophone	$24.95
(ELM04013)	E♭ Instruments—Alto and Baritone Saxophone	$24.95
(ELM04014)	B♭ Trumpet and Clarinet	$24.95
(ELM04015)	Bass Clef Instruments—Trombone, Baritone, Horn and Tuba	$24.95

also available from Bob Mintzer and Belwin Jazz:

The Music of Bob Mintzer: Solo Transcriptions and Performing Artist Master Class CD
Book & CD

(0479B)		$24.95

15 Easy Jazz, Blues & Funk Etudes
Book & CD

(ELM00029CD)	C Instruments—Flute, Guitar Keyboards	$19.95
(ELM00030CD)	B♭ Instruments Tenor Saxophone and Soprano Saxophone	$19.95
(ELM00031CD)	E♭ Instruments—Alto and Baritone Saxophone	$19.95
(ELM00033CD)	B♭ Trumpet and Clarinet	$19.95
(ELM00032CD)	Bass Clef Instruments—Trombone, Baritone, Horn and Tuba	$19.95

14 Blues & Funk Etudes
Book & CD

(EL9604CD)	C Instruments—Flute, Guitar Keyboards	$26.95
(EL9605CD)	B♭ Instruments Tenor Saxophone and Soprano Saxophone	$26.95
(EL9607CD)	E♭ Instruments—Alto and Baritone Saxophone	$26.95
(EL9606CD)	B♭ Trumpet	$26.95
(EL9608CD)	Bass Clef Instruments—Trombone, Baritone, Horn and Tuba	$26.95

14 Jazz & Funk Etudes
Book & CD

(EL03949)	C Instruments—Flute, Guitar Keyboards	$24.95
(EL03950)	B♭ Instruments Tenor Saxophone and Soprano Saxophone	$24.95
(EL03952)	E♭ Instruments—Alto and Baritone Saxophone	$24.95
(EL03951)	B♭ Trumpet	$24.95
(EL03953)	Bass Clef Instruments—Trombone, Baritone, Horn and Tuba	$24.95

Belwin JAZZ
a division of **Alfred**

All prices in US Dollars and subject to change
wo 538

ORDER MUSIC TODAY

Learn what you need, play what you want.
OrderMusicToday.com

Conquer theory fears with Alfred's
ESSENTIALS OF MUSIC THEORY

By Andrew Surmani, Karen Farnum Surmani, Morton Manus

The most complete music theory course ever!

This all-in-one series includes concise lessons with short exercises, ear-training activities and reviews. Available in three separate volumes or as a complete set, *Essentials of Music Theory* also includes Ear-Training CDs (performed by acoustic instruments), a Teacher's Answer Key Book, reproducible Teacher's Activity Kits, Bingo Games, Flash Cards and Computer Software. The Alto Clef edition includes primarily alto clef examples, with some treble and bass clef examples as well.

	Volume 1	Volume 2	Volume 3	Complete
BOOKS				
Student Book	(00-17231) $6.50	(00-17232) $6.50	(00-17233) $6.50	(00-17234) $12.50
Student Book w/2 Ear-Training CDs	——	——	——	(00-16486) $31.50
Student Book / Alto Clef (Viola) Edition	(00-18580) $6.50	(00-18581) $6.50	(00-18582) $6.50	(00-18583) $19.95
NEW! Student Book / Alto Clef w/2 Ear-Training CDs	——	——	——	(00-27642) $34.95
Teacher's Answer Key Book	——	——	——	(00-17256) $19.50
Teacher's Answer Key Book & 2 Ear-Training CDs	——	——	——	(00-17261) $37.50
EAR-TRAINING CDS				
Ear-Training CD		(00-17252) $10.95	(00-17253) $10.95	(00-17254) $18.95
DOUBLE BINGO GAMES				
NEW! Key Signature Double Bingo	——	——	——	(00-24448) $19.95
Note Naming Double Bingo	——	——	——	(00-19481) $19.95
Rhythm Double Bingo	——	——	——	(00-19479) $19.95
FLASH CARDS				
NEW! Key Signature Flash Cards	——	——	——	(00-24447) $9.95
Note Naming Flash Cards	——	——	——	(00-20320) $9.95
Rhythm Flash Cards	——	——	——	(00-19396) $9.95
TEACHER'S ACTIVITY KITS				
Teacher's Activity Kit	(00-19380) $19.95	(00-20373) $19.95	**NEW!** (00-26321) $19.95	**NEW!** (00-26327) $49.95
VERSION 2.0 SOFTWARE				
Student Version	(00-18827) $29.95	(00-20822) $39.95		(00-18833) $59.95
Educator Version	(00-18826) $99.95	(00-20821) $119.95		(00-18832) $199.95
Network Version (for 5 simultaneous users•)	(00-20322) $300.00	(00-20823) $350.00		(00-20321) $500.00

Which version do I need?

Student Version
- Ideal for individual students using the program one at a time
- Not necessary to track other users' progress

Educator Version
- Ideal for educators with one computer in a classroom, or for private lesson/studio use
- Educator has ability to track all users' progress & create custom tests

Network Version
- Includes all Educator Version features
- Designed for use on networked computers

•*Additional Network User Licenses can be purchased as follows:* **Volume 1—$20 each, Volumes 2 & 3—$25 each, Complete—$40 each**

Visit **alfred.com** and click on "Theory & Reference" for a handy interactive guide to help you decide which version is right for you.